A Martian Comes to Stay

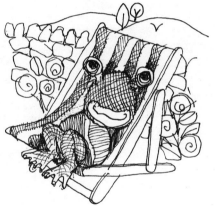

Written by Penelope Lively

Illustrated by Alison Bartlett

Hodder
Children's
Books

a division of Hodder Headline Limited

This story was first published in *Jubilee Jackanory* by the BBC in 1977.
It was then reprinted in Penelope Lively's story collection, *Uninvited Ghosts*,
published by William Heinemann in 1984, and then published as a
separate volume by Macdonald Young Books in 1995.

This new edition first published in Great Britain in 2002
by Hodder Children's Books

A Catalogue record for this book is available from the
British Library

ISBN 0 340 85568 1

Printed and bound in Great Britain by
Bookmarque Ltd., Croydon, Surrey

Hodder Children's Books
A division of Hodder Headline Limited
338 Euston Road, London NW1 3BH

Chapter One

It was on the second day of Peter's holiday with his grandmother that the Martian came to the cottage. There was a knock at the door and when he went to open it there was this small green person with webbed feet and eyes on the end of stumpy antennae who said, perfectly politely, "I wonder if I might bother you for the loan of a spanner?"

"Sure," said Peter. "I'll ask my gran."

Gran was in the back garden, it being a nice sunny day.

Peter said, "There's a Martian at the door who'd like to borrow a spanner."

Gran looked at him over her knitting. "Is there, dear? Have a look in Grandad's toolbox, there should be one there."

That's not what your grandmother would have said? No, nor mine either but Peter's gran was an unusual lady, as you will discover. Grandad had died a few years earlier and she lived alone in this isolated cottage in the country, growing vegetables and keeping chickens, and Peter liked going to stay with her more than almost anything he could think of.

Gran was not like most people. She was unflappable and what you might call open-minded, which accounts for everything that happened next.

Peter found the spanner and took it back to the Martian, who held out a rather oddly constructed hand and thanked him warmly.

"We've got some trouble with the gears or something and had to make an emergency landing. And now the mechanic says he left his tools back at base. I ask you! It's all a mystery to me — I'm just the steward. Anyway — thanks a lot. I'll bring it back in a minute." And he padded away up the lane.

There was no one around, but
then there wasn't likely to be: the cottage
was a quarter of a mile from the village
and hardly anyone came by except the
occasional farm tractor and the odd
holidaymaker who'd got lost. Peter
went back into the garden.

"Should have offered him a cup of tea," said Gran. "He'll have had a fair journey, I shouldn't wonder."

"Yes," said Peter. "I didn't think of that."

In precisely three minutes' time there was a knock at the door. The Martian was there, looking distinctly agitated. He said, "They've gone."

"Who's gone?" said Peter.

"The others. The spaceship. All of them. They've taken off and left me."

Gran, by now, had come through from the garden. She hitched her specs up her nose and looked down at the Martian, who was nearly three feet high.

"You'd best come in," she said, "while we have a think. Gone, you say? Where was it, this thing of yours?"

"Over there," said the Martian, pointing across the lane.

"Ah," said Gran. "Ted Thomas's field."

"The one with the bullocks in," added Peter.

"Bullocks?" said the Martian.

"Big brown animals," explained Peter.

"Animals?" said the Martian.

"Creatures that walk about and eat, like you and me, only different."

The Martian nodded. "I saw them, then. I hoped they were harmless."

"They are," said Peter.

"But curious," said Gran. "They'd have wanted to have a look at this space whatsit, wouldn't they? Stand round it in a circle, making heavy breathing noises. Would they be a bit jumpy, your friends, Mr, er . . . ?"

"Very," said the Martian. "We tend

to be, when we get off-course. I'm
dead jumpy right now. For one thing,
I'm frightened of that thing in the
corner that makes a ticking noise.
Is it going to blow up?"

Peter explained about clocks.

Gran, meanwhile, had put the kettle on. "The way I see it, these friends of Mr, er . . . looked out and saw Ted's bullocks and lost their heads, and who's to blame them? Still, it's not very nice, leaving him stuck here like this. I mean, it's not as though we can give the village taxi a ring and get him home like that. I don't know what's to be done for the best, I really don't. Meanwhile, we'll have a nice cup of tea."

Chapter Two

Tea and a couple of digestive biscuits cheered the Martian up. He sat on the footstool by the stove and apologized for being such a nuisance.

"Not at all," said Gran. "We don't get a lot of company round here. It's you I'm bothered about. But anyway, we've got the attic room empty so you're welcome to stop until we can work something out. You'll be company for Peter." She gazed for a moment at the visitor and went on, delicately, "Are you, er, young or old, as you might say?"

"I'm three hundred and twenty-seven," said the Martian.

"Ah," said Gran. "Then there's a bit of an age-gap, on the face of it. Peter's nine. Still, it's the spirit that counts, isn't it? That's what I always find, anyway."

The Martian was an adaptable visitor.

He felt the cold rather and preferred to sit
right up against the stove and once, with
further apologies, got into the oven for a
bit to warm up.

"Get a lot of sun, do you, where
you come from?" asked Gran.

But the Martian was rather vague about his home surroundings; it was different, he said – adding hastily that of course he didn't mean it was better.

Once or twice he looked out of the window nervously. He wanted to know why the trees kept moving.  "It's the wind, dear," said Gran, who tended to take people into the family once she liked them.

"They're not aggressive?"

"Not to speak of."

Later, they watched television. The Martian was interested but inclined to raise questions. "Is it true to life?" he enquired, in the middle of *Top of the Pops*.

"No," said Peter. "At least not most people's."

"What about this?" asked the Martian presently, when a soap opera was on.

"I wouldn't say so," said Gran. "But then I've had a limited experience."

He appreciated *Zoo Quest*, which was about South American creatures.

"That's Nature," said Gran. "It's very highly thought of nowadays. Time I got us something to eat." She looked doubtfully at the Martian. "You're not on a special diet or anything like that, I hope?"

But the Martian proved admirably easy to feed. He was a bit wary of sausages but discovered a passion for jam tarts.

"You tuck in," said Gran. "You'll be hungry, after that journey."

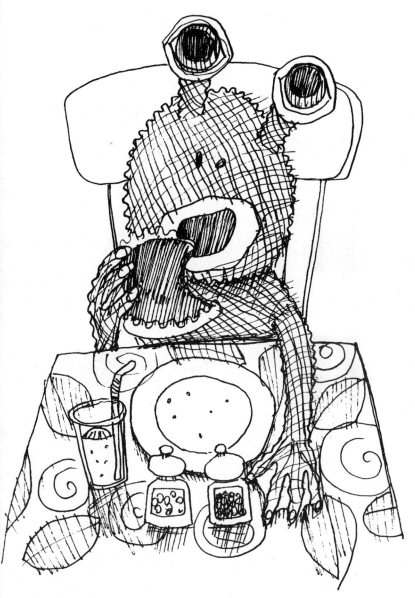

Chapter Three

Over the next couple of days the
Martian settled in nicely. He insisted
on helping with the washing-up and
played Monopoly with Peter. Peter
won every time, which he found
embarrassing. The Martian didn't seem
to grasp the idea of making money.

"I'm sorry," he said apologetically.
"Why do I want to have more and more
of these bits of paper?"

"So that you can buy things," Peter
explained.

"Things to eat?"

"Well, no. It's streets and hotels
and things, in the game."

"Mind," said Gran, "he's got a
point. It's something I've wondered
about myself. Maybe you should try a
game of cards."

They played Snap and Rummy
but this wasn't much better. The Martian
preferred not to win.

"To my mind," said Gran, "they've
got a different outlook on life, wherever
he comes from."

She was knitting the Martian a
sweater now.

"Would you come here a minute,
dear, just so I can measure it across
the chest."

The Martian stood in front of her
obligingly. Gran stretched the knitting
across his greenish, rather leathery body.

"It's to keep the chill out," she
went on. "Being as you feel the cold
so. I've no objection at all to a person
going around in the altogether if
that's what they're used to, let's get
that clear. There – that's a nice fit."

The Martian was quite embarrassingly
grateful.

He did not venture outside, which
seemed on the whole advisable in any case.

Neighbours in remote country districts
tend to be inquisitive about other
people's visitors and the Martian would
be an odd one to have to explain.

"I suppose," said Peter, "we could say he's a distant relative who's come from somewhere abroad."

"That's not going to satisfy some folks I could name," said Gran. "Not with him being as unusual-looking as he is. Even if we said he took after another branch of the family. No, it's best if he stays put till his friends come back. D'you think they'll take long, dear?"

The Martian shook his head doubtfully. He said he thought they would come, eventually, but that they might be having difficulty finding the right spot again.

"Well, not to worry," said Gran. "We'll just bide our time till they do."

After several days the Martian overcame his worries about trees and various noises that bothered him such as birds and dogs barking, and sat in a deckchair in the garden, wearing Gran's sweater and with a rug round him.

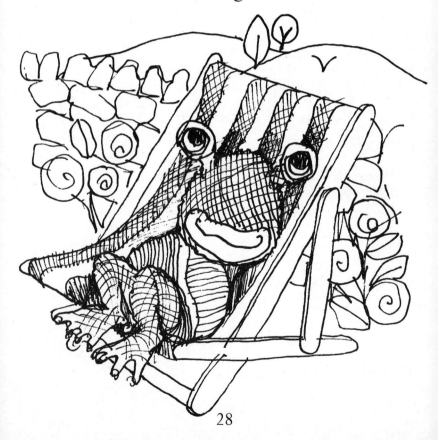

On one of these occasions old Mr Briggs from down the lane came past with his dog and stopped for a moment to chat to Gran over the wall.

"Ah," he said, glancing over her shoulder. "Got another of your grandchildren stopping with you, then?"

"In a manner of speaking," said Gran evasively.

Mr Biggs departed, calling over his shoulder, "See you at the village fête, Saturday."

Gran sat down again. "It's a shame we can't take him along to the fête. Be ever so interesting for him. I mean, it's what you want, when you're in foreign parts – have a look at how other people set about things. The Flower Show'll be a treat this year, with the good weather we've been having."

The Martian said wistfully that he would love to go.

"I wonder," said Gran. "Let's see now. S'pose we . . ."

And then Peter had a brilliant idea. In the cupboard under the stairs there was an old pushchair that had been used for him and his sister when they were small. If they put the Martian in that and covered him up with a pram-rug and put something round his head, he could pass for a small child.

Gran clapped her hands. "Clever boy! There now, we'll have ourselves an outing!"

The Martian beamed, if someone with antennae, a mouth somewhat like a letter-box and not much else by way of features can be said to beam.

"You know," Gran confided to Peter later on, when they were alone, "I've really took to him. You can tell he's been brought up nicely, from his manners. There's some human beings I know would be put to shame."

Chapter Four

The day of the fête was fine and dry.
The Martian was installed in the
pushchair, swathed in a blue rug that
Gran had crocheted a long time ago
and with an old pixie hood that had
belonged to Peter's sister on his head.

His antennae poked out through two holes, which did not look quite right, so they had to fix a sunshade to the handles of the pushchair and drape some muslin over this; in this way the Martian was only dimly visible as a muffled form.

"We'll say he's sensitive to sunstroke," said Gran, "if anyone gets nosy."

They set off for the village with the Martian in a pushchair.

The Martian was fascinated with everything he saw. He asked them to stop for him to admire the Amoco Garage with its swags of flapping plastic flags and brightly coloured signs about Four Star Petrol and Credit Cards Accepted. He found it, he declared, very beautiful.

"Well," said Gran doubtfully, "to my mind that's on the garish side, but I suppose it is a matter of taste."

The Martian said humbly that he probably hadn't been here long enough yet to be much of a judge of these things. He gazed at the display of baked bean tins and cornflakes packets in the window of the Minimarket and asked anxiously if that would be considered handsome.

"Not really," said Peter. "I mean, it's the sort of thing that's so ordinary you don't really notice."

"He's seeing a different angle to us," said Gran. "Stands to reason, when you think about it."

The smell of petrol made him sneeze. Mrs Lilly from the Post Office, who happened to be passing at the time, craned her head round to stare into the pushchair, "Bless its little heart, then! Tishoo!" She bent down. "Little boy or a little girl, is it?"

"Boy," said Gran. "I wouldn't be surprised if that cold wasn't giving way to something worse," she added loudly.

Mrs Lilly backed away.

Chapter Five

They reached the village green, on
which the fête was taking place.
The band was already playing.

The Martian peered out from
under the sunshade.

"Watch it!" said Peter warningly.
"People'll see you."

The Martian apologized. "It's just that it's all so exciting."

"We always put on a good show," said Gran modestly. "It's a question of upstaging Great Snoggington down the road, up to a point," she explained.

The Martian, under the sunshade, nodded.

Gran pointed out the vicar and the head teacher from the village school and Mr Soper who ran the pub.

"They are your leaders?" asked the Martian.

"In a manner of speaking," said Gran.

They toured the Bring and Buy stall and the Flower Tent. Gran paused to cast a professional eye over the sweet peas. Peter took out his money to see if he had enough left for another ice cream.

Neither of them saw Susie Stubbs, who was aged three and in Peter's opinion the most appalling brat in the village, sidle up to the pushchair. She put out a fat finger and poked the Martian, who sat perfectly still. Susie stuck her face under the sunshade.

There was an earsplitting shriek. Susie's mum, busy in the middle of a piece of juicy gossip with a friend, broke off and came rushing over.

"Ooooh . . .!" wailed Susie. "An 'orrible fing! An 'orrible fing like a snail! Oooh – I don't like it! Want to go home! Want my mum! Take it away! Ooh, an 'orrible fing in that pram!"

"There, my pet," cooed Susie's mum. "There, there . . . Did she have a nasty fright, then? Let's buy her an ice lolly, shall we?"

"'Orrible fing . . ." howled Susie, pointing at the pushchair.

Gran glared. She jerked the pushchair away, nearly dislodging the Martian.

"There now, my duckie," said
Susie's mum. "Why don't you ask the
little girl if she'd like to come and play,
then?"

"Boy," snapped Gran. "Pity he's
got such a shocking case of chicken-pox
or he'd have liked to, wouldn't you then,
Johnnie? 'Bye now, Mrs Stubbs."

An interested group of observers had gathered. Peter and Gran departed hastily.

"Sorry about that," said Gran to the Martian.

The Martian replied politely that where he came from also young people were sometimes inclined to be tiresome.

They left the Flower Tent, pausing for Gran to have a word with one or two friends. Curiosity, though, had now been aroused; people kept casting interested glances at the pushchair.

"That your Ron's youngest?" enquired Mrs Binns from the shop.

"Eh?" said Gran loudly; she was expert at producing sudden onsets of deafness when convenient.

Outside they sat down to watch the police dog display. One of the dogs, which was supposed to be tracking a man who was supposed to be an escaped criminal, kept rushing over and sniffing at the pushchair.

"Get away, you brute," snarled Gran.

The Martian, beneath the sunshade, kept bravely silent but had turned quite pale when Peter took a look at him.

He fetched some orange juice from the Refreshment Tent.

"Thank you," said the Martian faintly.

Chapter Six

A stout figure swathed in several
Indian bedspreads sat under a sign
which declared her to be . . .

Madame Rita,
the internationally
famous palmist
and fortune teller.

"That's
the
Vicar's
wife,"
said Gran.

"I'm not having her nosing around my future." Nevertheless, she veered in that direction.

The Vicar's wife, her face blotted out by an enormous pair of sunglasses, seized Gran's hand and predicted a tall dark stranger next Thursday.

"That'll be him that comes to read the meter," said Gran. "Well-built, I'd call him rather than tall, but never mind."

The Vicar's wife, bending down, lifted the muslin draped over the Martian's sunshade.

"What about the baby, then – let's have your hand, duckie." She gave a gasp of horror. "Oh, my goodness, the poor little dear, whatever . . ."

"Whatever what?" said Gran frostily.

The Vicar's wife dropped the muslin. "Well, he's a nice little thing, of course, but . . . well . . . unusual."

Gran gave her a withering look. "I'd say those specs you've got on aren't doing you any good, Mrs Mervyn. Fashionable they may be but not what I'd call serviceable. Well, I'd best be getting on."

"Whew!" said Peter, when they were out of earshot. "It's getting a bit dodgy here."

Gran agreed. "Anyway, he's seen a bit of our way of life, that's the main thing. We'll get home now."

But the damage had been done. There was gossip. The village had been alerted. The next day, three people turned up at the cottage declaring that they happened to be passing and hadn't seen Gran for a month of Sundays and had been wondering how she was.

Gran managed to get rid of them all. The Martian sat by the stove saying sadly that he was afraid he was becoming a problem.

"It's not you that's the problem," said Gran. "It's human nature."

All the same, they realized that he could not stay there for ever.

"At least not without us becoming world famous," said Peter. "And him being put on the telly and that kind of thing."

"I shouldn't care for that," said the Martian in alarm. "I'm basically very shy."

They discussed what was to be done. The Martian said that he thought that probably his companions would be trying to find the spot at which they had landed but were having navigational problems.

"Anything you can think of we could do to lend a hand?" enquired Gran.

"We could signal," said Peter. "In their language. He could tell us what to say."

The Martian became quite excited. He'd need some kind of radio transmitter, he said.

Gran shook her head. "I've not got one of those to hand. But there's Jim's big torch up in the attic. We could flash that, like, when it's dark."

Chapter Seven

They had their first signal session
that evening. The Martian dictated
a series of long and short flashes and
Peter and Gran took it in turns to
stand at the window with the lights
off, waving the torch at the sky.

Gran thoroughly enjoyed it. She wanted to put in all sorts of extras like invitations to tea and enquiries about whether they preferred fruit cake or a nice jam sponge.

She hoped there wouldn't be misunderstandings. "We don't want one of them satellites coming down in Ted Thomas's field. Or a bunch of them RAF blokes."

But nothing happened. They decided to try again the next night.

They had been at it for an hour or two – with a break to watch *Coronation Street*, to which the Martian was becoming dangerously addicted – when there was a knock at the door.

"Oh, it's you, Bert," said Gran. "What's up, then? Don't you start telling me I've got no telly licence, because I have. Top drawer of the dresser, have a look for yourself."

The village policeman was standing there. He said heavily, "I'm obliged to ask you if I might come in and look round the premises, Mrs Tranter."

"What's all this posh talk for?" said Gran. "Come on in. Help yourself." She put the torch on the table.

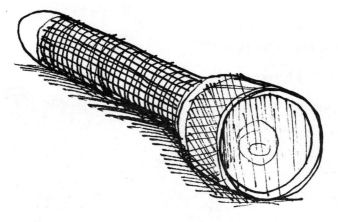

The policeman eyed it. "Would you mind telling me what you've been using that implement for, Mrs Tranter?"

"That," snapped Gran, "is a torch,

and if you don't know what torches
are for, Bert Davies, then you'll never
make sergeant, frankly."

The policeman, a little red now
around the neck, met Gran's glare
valiantly, eyeball to eyeball.

"Would you by any chance, Mrs
Tranter, have been passing information
to a foreign power?"

There was
an awful silence.
Peter and the
Martian, who
was cowering
behind the
stove,
exchanged
nervous glances.

"Bert Davies," said Gran at last, "I've known you since you was in nappies. You come here asking that kind of thing once more – just once more – and I'm off down the village to have a word with your mum." She glared at the policeman, who was now a rich strawberry colour to the roots of his hair, and was backing towards the door.

"There's been reports," he said. "Reports about flashing lights and that. It's my duty to investigate."

"It's your duty to get back to the village and see about them motor bike boys that's always charging through over the speed limit," snapped Gran.

It was at that moment that Peter heard a curious whirring noise from somewhere outside.

The policeman, mercifully, was too
unnerved to pay any attention, if indeed

he had heard
anything; he
retreated to his car,
with as much dignity
as he could manage,

and drove off into the night . . .

. . . at precisely the same time as
something brightly-spiced with lights

loomed above
Ted Thomas's
field, hovered for
a moment, and
sank below the
line of the hedge.

Peter cried, "They're here!"

"And none before time too," said Gran.

The Martian was already on his feet and hurrying to the door. He paused, trying to take off his sweater.

"You keep that," said Gran. "Someone might like to copy the pattern, up where you come from."

The Martian held out his hand. "Thank you very much for having me. I've enjoyed it enormously. I wish I could suggest . . ." He hesitated.

"No, dear," said Gran. "Return visits are out, I'm afraid. Foreign travel doesn't appeal to me nowadays. A week in Llandudno in August does me nicely."

From the field, there was still that whirring noise, and a shimmering orange glow.

"Better go," said Peter anxiously,

"before anyone comes."

The Martian nodded. He padded out and down the lane. They saw him get smaller and more indistinct and turn in at the gate into the field and then the orange glow got larger and the whirring got louder and there was a snap of bright lights and a rush and then silence and darkness.

Gran closed the door. "That, I take it," she said, "was one of them flying saucers. Pity we couldn't have taken a picture. It would have been nice for my album.

"Put the torch back in the attic, would you, dear. And put that spanner back in your grandad's toolbox, while you're at it. Good thing we had that by us, or we'd never have been able to lend a hand in the first place. I should have made him up some sandwiches for the journey, you know."

And she settled down by the stove with her knitting.

h *More fast and funny fiction for independent readers from Hodder Children's Books . . .*

A Martian in the Supermarket

Written by Penelope Lively
Illustrated by Alison Bartlett

Judy first sees the Martian when her mum's looking for fish fingers. *She* isn't scared, but he's a bit nervous. His rocket's engine won't start, so Judy take him back to her house. They soon become good friends. But when the Martian gets homesick, can Judy help to get the rocket fixed, and set the Martian free?